The Boy Who Didn't Believe
IN CHRISTMAS

BY MICHAEL TEITELBAUM

ILLUSTRATED BY BARBARA STEADMAN

GROSSET & DUNLAP, NEW YORK

A Division of The Putnam Publishing Group

Copyright © 1985 by Calash Corporation N.V. All rights reserved. SANTA CLAUS, THE MOVIE is a trademark of Calash Corporation and licensed by Merchandising Corporation of America, Inc. Published by Grosset & Dunlap, a member of The Putnam Publishing Group, New York. Published simultaneously in Canada. Printed in Italy. Library of Congress Catalog Card Number 85-70660   ISBN 0-448-10277-3
A B C D E F G H I J

Joe was a boy who had no family. Joe was a boy who had no friends. Joe did not even have a warm place to stay on a cold December night.

This particular December night was Christmas Eve, but that meant nothing to Joe. When he saw Christmas treats in store windows, he felt hungry. When he saw people hurrying home with Christmas packages, he felt lonely.

Joe was a boy who didn't believe in Christmas—or Santa Claus.

Joe walked along the city streets. By and by he saw a girl in the window of a townhouse.

Wouldn't it be wonderful, he thought, if he could be the child who lived in that house! What a delicious Christmas dinner he would have! Suddenly Joe realized that the girl in the window was staring at him.

The girl in the window was named Cornelia. She lived with an uncle she rarely saw. Miss Tucker, the nanny, took care of Cornelia.

It was true that Cornelia was having a delicious Christmas dinner. It was true that she had many nice things. But in one way she was just like Joe.

She was lonely, too.

"Cornelia! Come away from that window this instant before you get a draft!" said Miss Tucker.

Cornelia glanced once more at the boy in the street before she went back to the table. She wasn't very hungry. It was not much fun spending Christmas Eve with a nanny.

"That boy looked cold," Cornelia thought. "I wonder if he's hungry."

When Miss Tucker left the room, Cornelia put some food on a plate. Then she tiptoed through the kitchen to the door.

When she opened the door, she saw that the boy was still standing on the sidewalk.

"Psssssst!" she whispered in the dark. "Hey, little boy!"

Joe stared at Cornelia, but he didn't say anything. He watched her set the plate of food on the step.

When Cornelia went back into the house, Joe decided it was safe to move. He walked quietly to the step, sat down, and ate everything on the plate.

He didn't know that Cornelia was standing on the other side of the door, listening. She wished that she and the boy outside could be friends, but she knew that wishing could not always make things happen.

As soon as he finished eating, Joe left. He felt much better now that he had had some dinner.

As he walked along, he thought about the girl who lived in the townhouse. She seemed very nice. He wished that he and she could be friends, but Joe knew that wishing could not always make things happen.

But what Joe and Cornelia did not remember was that on one night of the year—Christmas Eve—there is someone who wants to make children happy. While millions of boys and girls lie sleeping, Santa Claus is flying through the sky with a sleigh full of toys.

When Santa Claus came that night to the city where Joe and Cornelia lived, he was feeling very jolly.

"Ho-ho-ho!" he laughed. "What a night! Lights in the windows, stockings hung by the fireplaces! I bet there isn't a child alive who isn't filled with the joy of Christmas."

Then Santa happened to see Joe. Here was a boy who was not filled with the joy of Christmas. Here was a boy who was not even in bed. Joe was huddled in a doorway, trying to stay warm.

"Just a minute!" said Santa. "I think I'll make an unscheduled stop."

Joe was just noticing that the wind was growing colder when he saw what looked to him like a man in a Santa costume.

"What are you doing out here?" the man asked.

The man's voice was very kind, but Joe was suspicious.

"Hey! Get out of here!" said Joe. "Find your own doorway."

"Don't you know who I am?" the man asked. "I'm Santa Claus."

"Oh, yeah," said Joe rudely. "And I'm the Tooth Fairy."

"Don't you recognize my clothes?" said Santa.

"Anyone can rent a costume," said Joe.

"Hmmmm," said Santa. "I guess I'll just have to prove this my way."

Suddenly there was a WHOOSH and Joe and Santa appeared on
the nearby rooftop. Joe found himself staring at a sleigh and eight
beautiful reindeer.

"This is my sleigh," Santa explained. "Would you like to go for a
ride?"

Some of the reindeer looked up at Joe, waiting to hear his answer.

"The two in the lead are Donner and Blitzen," said Santa.

Santa helped Joe climb into the sleigh, and then he sat down beside him. They sat there for a few moments, saying nothing.

"When you're ready to go, just say YO!" Santa said.

"YO!" cried Joe.

At once, eight reindeer leaped into the air and off they flew.

Joe was now bursting with excitement. He was really flying. He was really sitting next to Santa Claus. It was really Christmas Eve.

He looked over the edge of the sleigh and saw the city below them.

"Wow!" said Joe. That was all he could say.

"Would you like to hold the reins?" Santa asked him.

While Joe held on to the reins, Santa gave him instructions.
"Pull them both together to go higher.
"Pull on the left rein to go left...
"...and the right rein to go right."
"On Donner, on Blitzen!" cried Joe.
"Well, Joe," Santa said after awhile. "Just set the sleigh down on that townhouse roof over there. I have to make a delivery."
Joe guided the reindeer down to the roof. They landed gracefully.
"The girl who lives here wrote to me and said that the only thing she needed was a friend," said Santa.

They both stepped out of the sleigh. Santa put his sack over his shoulder.

"Would you like to come down the chimney with me?" he asked.

Joe said he would, and down the chimney they went.

"Remember," said Santa, as they were going down. "Be quiet."

When they came into the living room, it was dark. Joe bumped into a table and knocked over a lamp. The lamp went crashing to the floor.

Someone heard the crash and came to see what was going on in the living room. It was the girl who lived there.

When she saw Santa Claus, she gasped.

"Are you *him?*" she cried. "Are you really Santa Claus?"

Then the girl looked at Joe. Joe looked at the girl.

"You're the boy in the street," the girl cried.

"You're the girl in the window," said Joe.

"Hmmmm," said Santa. "You two seem to know each other."

"My name is Cornelia," said the girl, "but you can call me Corny."

"My name is Joe," said Joe. "You can call me Joe."

"Are we going to be friends?" Cornelia asked.

"I think so," said Joe. "Everything else that happened tonight was wonderful."

Santa looked at them. "Well, I have more stops to make," he said. "I guess I'll be going."

"Will I ever see you again?" asked Joe.

"Of course," said Santa, with a smile.

Cornelia and Joe did become friends, and they went on to have
many adventures together. They saw Santa again, just as Santa
predicted. He had brought them together. He gave each of them what
each most wished for—a friend.

Sometimes friendship can be the best gift of all!